FERRY BOAT

Michael Garland

I Like to Read®
HOLIDAY HOUSE • NEW YORK

We go up.

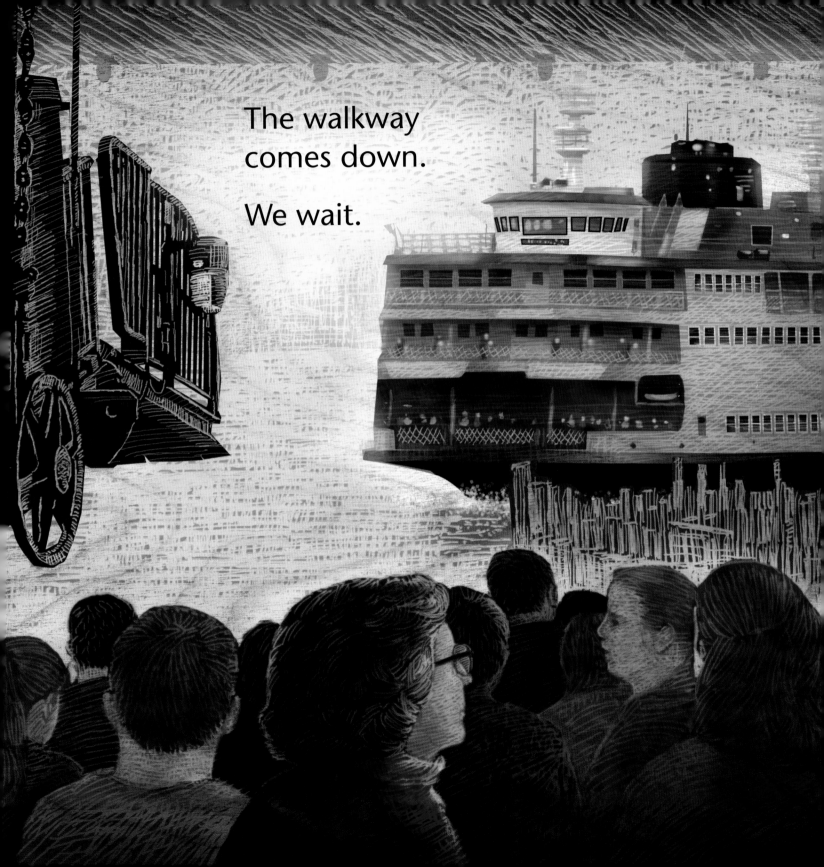

The walkway
comes down.

We wait.

We go on the ferry.

Let's go to the window.

Good-bye, Manhattan!

We see an island.

We see a fort.

We see a long, long bridge.

One day people saw a whale.
We do not see a whale today.

We do see the Statue of Liberty.

The ferry stops.
We are in Staten Island.

Some people go home.
Some people go to work.
Some people just go back again.

We buy something for Grandpa.

And we go back.
Hello, Manhattan!

Walkway

Ellis Island

Castle Williams

Verrazzano Bridge

Statue of Liberty